DRAGO

by Angie Belcher

PHOTOGRAPHY BY ANDY BELCHER

RAINBOW READING

When Eli showed me the entry form for the Birdman Competition I said, "You've got to be joking!"

But, as usual, I let him talk me into another of his crazy schemes.

BIRDMAN COMPETITION

Prizes for the longest flight, highest flight and most creative flying machine.

- All entrants must arrive by 1.30pm.

- Entrants will launch their craft off a flat platform jutting off Pilot Bay jetty.

- Entries must be people powered only.

- Only one person must fly but others can assist.

- Divers will be in the water to help retrieve debris and provide assistance if entrants get into trouble.

- The judges' decision will be final.

We called in a few of our friends to help and we gathered around our kitchen table. Eli produced a pen and a sheet of paper. We had a brainstorming session with Eli writing as quickly as he could while everyone called out his or her ideas.

First, we listed things that fly: a helicopter, airplanes, insects, birds, rockets, fish.

Next, we wrote a list of things that help objects fly: propellers, canopies, wings, and booster rockets. The list grew and grew then Eli drew it up as a mind map.

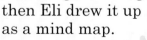

"What now?" I asked.
"Now we need to do a bit of research," Eli said.

Sophie went to the computer
and began searching the Internet
for articles about flight.

Toby went to the library
and found some books.

Jill rang her Uncle Steve
who was a pilot.

I started gathering up
all sorts of stuff from the
recycle pile.

This project was starting
to get exciting.

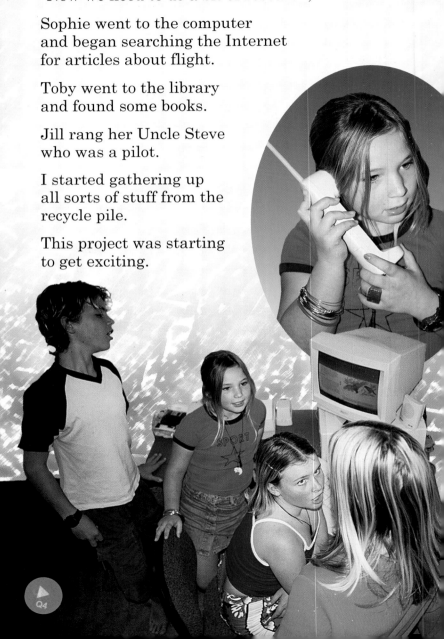

"What did you find out?" I asked Toby at the next meeting.

"I read that in ancient times the only flying things that people saw were birds and insects," he said. "Myths and legends were written about flight. One story told me about a Greek guy named Icarus. He glued wings onto himself to help escape from a prison. But he flew too close to the sun and the wax on the wings melted."

"Wow," I exclaimed.

"What did you find out, Sophie?"

She told us that a lot of brave and crazy people had tried to fly. An Englishman called Thomas Pelling became a local celebrity trying to fly but he died when he jumped off a church tower and the rope attached to him broke!

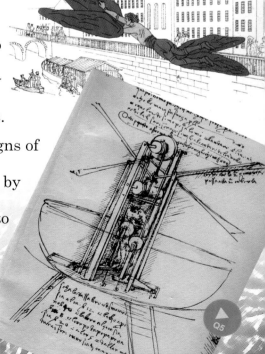

The Marquis de Bacqueville tried to fly using wings that looked like lily pads attached to his hands and feet.

Sophie found designs of helicopters and parachutes drawn by Leonardo da Vinci and pictures of Otto Lilienthal who flew the first glider.

Eli started drawing his own designs.
"Hey, I like that dragonfly," I told him, "But will it fly?"
"It's got wings and a couple of propellers," he said. "That's a good start."

We went outside and looked at all the scraps. There were old flyscreens, wire, ropes, belts, boards, material, wool, nails and needles.

Toby made some wings out of the old flyscreens and wire. We glued, stitched and tied all sorts of beautiful things onto the wings to make them sparkle and shine like real dragonfly wings. I wasn't sure if it would fly but it sure looked creative.

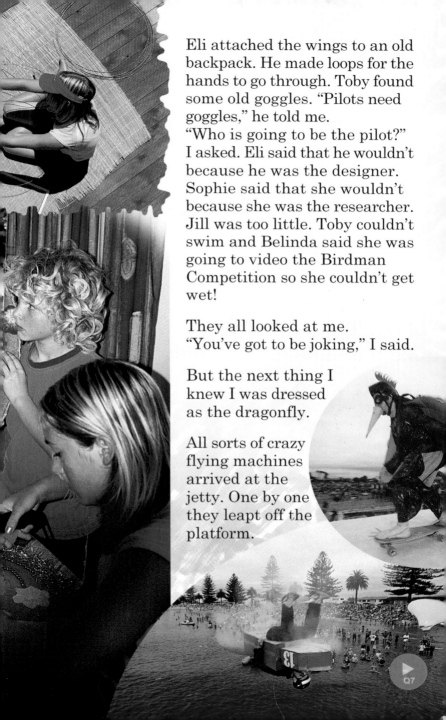

Eli attached the wings to an old backpack. He made loops for the hands to go through. Toby found some old goggles. "Pilots need goggles," he told me.
"Who is going to be the pilot?" I asked. Eli said that he wouldn't because he was the designer. Sophie said that she wouldn't because she was the researcher. Jill was too little. Toby couldn't swim and Belinda said she was going to video the Birdman Competition so she couldn't get wet!

They all looked at me.
"You've got to be joking," I said.

But the next thing I knew I was dressed as the dragonfly.

All sorts of crazy flying machines arrived at the jetty. One by one they leapt off the platform.

My heart was beating like crazy when it was my turn.

I smiled at the hundreds of people lining the beach. Then, looking straight ahead, I flapped my wings and ran as fast as I could.

Dragonfly?
More like Dragonflop!